CARMEN

By **Margarita del Mazo**   Illustrated by **Concha Pasamar**

To those who fight dragons to remember that they can fly.
—Margarita del Mazo and Concha Pasamar

I'm nine years old. I have a ball that I always carry around with me, and a friend who's a corporal in the Dragon Regiment of Alcalá.

He is a real dragon, but doesn't really look like one. He's very much in command, and when he gives an order, everyone snaps to attention. Maybe they're afraid he's going to breathe fire on them! He's three heads taller than me, and he wears a uniform that's so neat it shines in the dark.

People call him Don José. Only important people are called Don. As far as I know, nobody in my family is called Don. And my mom and dad are the most important people in the world to me.

Compañía Nacional de Danza

GOBIERNO DE ESPAÑA · MINISTERIO DE CULTURA Y DEPORTE · **inaem** INSTITUTO NACIONAL DE LAS ARTES ESCÉNICAS Y DE LA MÚSICA

This picture book is the result of a collaboration and partnership between the Spanish National Dance Company and Cuento de Luz.

We share dreams, a love for the performing arts, and the same philosophy of spreading human and universal values.

We hope that young and old readers from many corners of the world will be moved after reading it and embrace with their hearts the wonderful world of dance.

Ana Eulate
Cuento de Luz
cuentodeluz.com

Joaquín De Luz
Spanish National Dance Company
cndanza.mcu.es/en

This book is printed on **Stone Paper** that is **Silver Cradle to Cradle Certified®**.

Cradle to Cradle™ is one of the most demanding ecological certification systems, awarded to products that have been conceived and designed in an ecologically intelligent way.

Cuento de Luz™ became a **Certified B Corporation** in 2015. The prestigious certification is awarded to companies that use the power of business to solve social and environmental problems and meet higher standards of social and environmental performance, transparency, and accountability.

Carmen
Text © 2022 by Margarita del Mazo
Illustrations © 2022 by Concha Pasamar
© 2022 Compañía Nacional de Danza INAEM
© 2022 Cuento de Luz SL
Calle Claveles, 10 | Pozuelo de Alarcón | 28223 | Madrid | Spain
Original title in Spanish: *Carmen*
English translation by Jon Brokenbrow
ISBN: 978-84-18302-76-3
1st printing
Printed in PRC by Shanghai Cheng Printing Company, March 2022, print number 1852-4

Don José isn't from around here. He came from far away to sort things out in my neighborhood, where people are always getting in trouble and fighting over everything. I don't like fighting at all, and that's why I like Don José. I get into fights only if people try to take my ball from me. Unless it's my dad: I don't fight with him, because he always wins. But it's my ball, and nobody else's.

When I grow up, I want to be like Don José, even if I don't have "Don" in front of my name. Maybe I can get it if I make a lot of money. Dad says money can buy anything.

I'll wear a uniform just like Don José's. And not even my dad will be able to take my ball off me.

Don José is a guard, and his job is very difficult. He can't even move to go to the bathroom.

I practice every day.

Don José is often in my neighborhood.

Well, sometimes the whole army shows up. People here don't behave the way they should.

The guards come to catch the smugglers who live here. People say you can earn a lot of money smuggling. I don't know where you go to study that, but I'm not interested, because they spend more time sleeping in prison than at home.

One day, one of them took my ball from me.

"Come and get it if you want it, squirt!" he said.

I strode up to him, but he pushed me to the ground. So I bit him. He let go of my ball and yelled so loudly people in the factory could hear him.

Don José smiled as he gave me the ball.

And he dragged off the smuggler, who was still yelling.

That day, Don José became my friend for life.

In the city where I live, there's a tobacco factory. It's the biggest building you could ever imagine. People say there isn't another one like it in the whole wide world. And the world is very big.

All the women who work in the factory are called cigarette girls because they make the cigarettes that other people smoke. My mom says that people who smoke ruin their lungs.

My neighbor Carmen is a cigarette girl.

Carmen is the most beautiful girl I know, and when I grow up, I'm going to marry her, even though she doesn't know it yet.

Sometimes I go to meet her when she leaves the factory. When the siren blows, the square fills up with boys who are waiting for her. They're all in love with her.

"Love me!"

"I'll take you to the very top!"

"Come with me!"

Carmen always sings them something that I know by heart:

> *Love is a rebellious bird*
> *that no one can tame,*
> *and if you call for it, it'll be quite in vain,*
> *for it's in its nature to say no.*

What it means is that she's just fine in the open air and that she can go wherever she likes, just like the birds.

Then she laughs, because she's always happy, and the sound of her laughter rings like the bells in the belfry. And she dances with one boy, then another, then another, then on her own, and then with another one again. She dances so well you just can't look away. The square is much prettier with Carmen in it.

Dad says she's saucy. But so is gazpacho, and I love it, nearly as much as my neighbor.

One afternoon she suddenly stops dancing.

Don José is on guard duty. Carmen walks toward him, singing. She walks around him, caresses his cheek, and throws him a flower.

He doesn't move a muscle.

Being on guard duty is very serious business. You have to be as still as you can, as if you are dead.

Carmen walks away without taking her eyes off him. And the square becomes as silent as a tomb.

Then the corporal does something he shouldn't have.

He looks all around him and picks up the flower. He breathes in its scent until it fills him completely, and then he puts it away.

He shouldn't have done that. He shouldn't have forgotten that he is on guard duty.

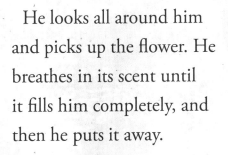

The next day there is a big fight in the factory. When Mom comes home, she says that there was a lot of shouting.

And that everyone gathered in a circle, and that nobody tried to stop it, because everyone wanted some entertainment.

Just like the circus!

And they cheered them on.

And someone yelled:

"Cut her!"

And then Carmen cut the other girl.

Grandpa sometimes cuts his cows' ears, but I don't think people should go around cutting other people. It hurts, and you're always left with a scar.

Mom says that she went to fetch the guards and that Don José took Carmen away.

I feel very sad for the girl who was cut.

And for Carmen as well.

Mom says that the corporal's face changed when he took hold of Carmen, and that he began to tremble.

"Oh, the heart…," she sighs. "Another one who's fallen in love with that girl. Poor thing!"

I know that when you fall in love, you give everything to the person you love, and you're left with nothing, and that's why you become poor. What I didn't know is that love makes you tremble. I imagine your heart beats so fast that your whole body shakes. That's what I've felt. It beats so hard that it leaps into your throat, and you have to clamp your jaws shut so it doesn't escape.

It seems that Carmen whispered things
into his ear, and Don José let her go.
That's why they've arrested him.

Now I feel sad for my friend.

I haven't seen my neighbor in a while. And I don't know anything about what happened to Don José.

For lunch, we are having gazpacho. I am on my third bowl when Dad comes home. Mom scolds him:

"You're late."

Dad says he was at the tavern.

"You'll never guess who showed up there. Our little neighbor, the man-eater."

"Dad! Carmen eats men?" I ask, terrified, although feeling kind of glad I am only a kid.

"Be quiet, boy! Don't talk nonsense!" says my dad.

And he keeps talking to my mother as if I'm not there, ignoring me completely. Grown-ups do that a lot when they don't know what to say.

"And what was she doing there?" asks my mom.

"Same as always. She came in hanging off the arm of a guard and left wrapped around a bullfighter."

While they talk about Carmen, I have another bowl of gazpacho and think about how they don't know anything about birds or freedom.

After lunch, while I'm washing my hands, I hear my dad say that the corporal also came into the tavern. I'm glad to know he'd been let go.

"Now, that guy's totally wild about Carmen," says my dad as he sits down in his chair.

I poke my head through the door.

"Being wild isn't good, is it, Dad?" I ask.

"Not good at all, son," says my dad.

"Not even a tiny bit?" I say.

"Not even a tiny bit," he says. "What's gotten into you today?"

But I ignore him so he can see just how bad I feel. I dry my hands, grab my ball, say "Goodbye" very quietly, and run out the door as fast as I can.

Someone I know needs a friend.

When I reach the tavern, Don José is outside, on his own. The wall is helping him stay upright. He is staring blankly ahead, like he's looking at a ghost. It's as if his body is right there, but he's gone a long way away.

I know what that's like, because it's exactly what happens to me in math class. The teacher helps me come back.

I think I should do the same with my friend. I say "Hi" to him a few times, but he doesn't answer. "Don José, are you drunk?" I ask.

He replies as if he's speaking from the bottom of a well.

"Yes! Drunk on love!" he says.

LILLAS

PASTIA

That must be the worst kind of drunk, because I've never seen anyone that bad before.

"I brought my ball. Shall we play?" I ask him.

He doesn't reply.

He puts his hands over his ears and suddenly yells a name.

"Carmen!"

And he yells it over and over again.

He sees her everywhere, in every face. When someone loves you, the way they say your name is different. You know that your name is safe in their mouth. But in this case, this isn't what I feel.

I hope Carmen's name leaves his mouth forever.

While he is wandering back and forth, shouting her name, and while I'm following him, waiting for him to say it for the last time, Carmen suddenly appears, holding on to another man's arm.

She is laughing as always, and she is more beautiful than ever.

That is when the dragon appears. It is really, really scary. It opens its jaws and spits out a great ball of fire.

The man drops to the ground like a sack of potatoes. I've never seen anything quite like it.

The dragon disappears, and Don José runs and runs and runs. I'm sure he is running away from the guards, but I think he is also running away from that terrible dragon.

The sudden blast makes me drop the ball. I never want to hear that sound again, but it's stuck inside my head. I run all the way home, fling my arms around my mom, and burst out crying.

The corporal has disappeared without a trace.

People say they've seen him in the hills, hiding in caves and eating all sorts of creatures.

I'm sure his heart is as black as coal. Now he's really alone.

I'm sure he'll never be able to rest, worrying that the guards are coming for him. And he won't be able to sleep at night.

I'm sure he's just as scared as I am, worrying that the dragon's going to come back.

That was all a while ago.

Carmen is still the most beautiful, joyful woman I know. Now she's the girlfriend of the most famous guy in the city.

It's no surprise that she fell for him, because he wears a glittering bullfighter's suit. There's no way you can miss it.

Today there's a bullfight. On those days I go over to the square and watch the crowd coming out of the bullring.

I can hear the cheering and applause inside.

When the bullfighter puts on a good show, the crowd carries him out on their shoulders. It's a fun game for him.

I think I see my neighbor far off in the distance.

I go over to say hi to her, but someone else gets there before me. He grabs her by the hands and pulls her until she falls to the ground.

The dragon is back!

Carmen tries to struggle free, but the beast's hands are grasped tightly around her wrists like shackles.

Frozen with fear, I think that the creature feels the same way about Carmen as I do about my ball.
He doesn't want anyone else to have her.
He doesn't want to share her.
He doesn't want her to be a bird.
He doesn't want her to be free.
He doesn't want her to be what she wants to be.
He just doesn't want her to be. And that is that.

"People don't have owners!" I yell.

Everything happens very quickly. The bird wants to fly away, and the beast finishes her off forever and ever.

I haven't gone back to admire the guards. I'm not interested anymore.

I haven't been to the square outside the factory, either.

I don't want to see Don José ever again.
I don't want to be his friend ever again.
I don't want to be like him.
I don't want "Don" in front of my name.
I don't want to see any more dragons.

They know nothing about love.